MY FAT... FLYING MACHINE

F. WARNE & Co

Peter Rabbit TV series imagery © Frederick Warne & Co. Ltd & Silvergate PPL Ltd, 2015.
Text, layout, and design © Frederick Warne & Co. Ltd, 2015.
The *Peter Rabbit* TV series is based on the works of Beatrix Potter. Peter Rabbit™ & Beatrix Potter™ Frederick Warne & Co.
Frederick Warne & Co. is the owner of all rights, copyrights, and trademarks in the Beatrix Potter character names and illustrations.
Published by the Penguin Group. Penguin Group (USA) LLC, 375 Hudson Street, New York, New York 10014, USA.
www.penguin.com A Penguin Random House Company
Manufactured in China.

978-0-7232-9564-8   10 9 8 7 6 5 4 3 2 1

Map of My Woods

This is a map of the woods where I live. You can see who else lives here, too. It's in my dad's journal, which I always have with me.

ROCKY ISLAND

OLD BROWN'S ISLAND

MR. JEREMY FISHER'S POND

SQUIRREL NUTKIN'S WOOD

MRS. TIGGY-WINKLE'S LAUNDRY

Jeremy Fisher is a clever and talented frog.

My mom— Mrs. Rabbit to you! I try to stay on her good side.

Mr. Bouncer is Benjamin's dad and a brilliant inventor.

Cotton-tail is my littlest sister, and the cutest!

JEMIMA PUDDLE-DUCK'S HILLTOP FARM

MR. McGREGOR'S GARDEN

My friend, **Lily Bobtail**. Whatever the problem, she's got the answer.

MR. TOD & TOMMY BROCK'S WOOD

MY BURROW

DR. & MRS. BOBTAIL'S BURROW (LILY'S HOME)

TUNNEL NETWORK

MR. BOUNCER'S BURROW (BENJAMIN'S HOME)

RAVINE

Benjamin Bunny is my cousin. Whatever I do, he's right behind me—usually hiding!

DEEP DARK WOODS

DANDELION FIELD

One sunny morning, Jeremy Fisher and Mr. Bouncer were telling Peter, Benjamin, and Lily all about the adventures they'd had with Peter's dad when they were young.

"Oh, those were the days!" laughed Mr. Bouncer.

"We were quite a team," agreed Jeremy Fisher.

Just then,
Peter spotted an old
photograph of his dad standing
next to something interesting.

"Wow, what's that?"

he asked.

"Aha, that was my
GREATEST INVENTION."
Mr. Bouncer smiled.
"A flying machine!
But your father
crash-landed in
Mr. McGregor's
garden and the
machine was never
seen again . . ."

Suddenly Peter had
a tip-top idea!

"Come on, we've got to find Dad's flying machine!"
said Peter. The three friends sneaked into Mr. McGregor's garden.
They searched high and low, but . . .

"There's no sign of it anywhere," sighed Benjamin.

"Sorry, Peter," said Lily.

"My dad always said, 'A good rabbit never gives up!'" said Peter. "Wait a minute," he gasped, spotting something among the vegetables. "That sign looks just like this part of the machine!"

Lily pointed to the photo.

"Look! Over by the beans," she said.

"There's another part!"

"And there's a wing!"
cried Benjamin, pointing.

As the friends looked around them, they spotted parts of the flying machine all over the garden!

"Now we just have to put it back together!" Peter said, smiling. But then . . .

CREAK! "Quick, hide!" whispered Peter as the farmhouse door opened and Mr. McGregor came out.

"Let's g-g-get out of here!" whispered Benjamin.

"We **CAN'T** give up now!" said Peter. "Lily, we can get the parts, and Benjamin, you can put them together. Let's hop to it!"

Peter and Lily crept carefully through the flowerbeds, tiptoed around the vegetables, and climbed up high to find all the pieces of the flying machine.

"Got it!"

exclaimed Lily, grabbing the central pole.

"Hmm, this part goes here . . .
that part goes there," said Benjamin,
cleverly fitting all the different pieces together.

The flying
machine was
almost complete
when . . .

"RABBITS!"
howled Mr. McGregor.
They'd been spotted!

"Let's get out of here,"
said Peter. "Help me spin the wings!"

The friends tried but nothing happened.

"We need a handle," cried Benjamin.
"Or we are not
going anywhere!"

"I know just the thing!"
said Peter.

He jumped onto a wheelbarrow, crept up behind Mr. McGregor, and then LEAPED to his pocket, grabbing his pencil!

"I'll put you in a pie!" roared Mr. McGregor.

But Peter was too fast.

"Try this!" yelled Peter, throwing the
pencil to Benjamin, who slotted it into place.

"It's now or never!" gasped Lily.

The three friends turned the
handle as fast as they
could and . . . just in time,
the flying machine took to the air!

"YIPPEE!"

cried Peter as they soared up and
over the garden wall, leaving a
very surprised Mr. McGregor still
standing among the vegetables.

Peter, Lily, and Benjamin flew
high over the woods.

"Peter, FLY!"

called Cotton-tail, spotting them
from outside the burrow.

"Peter Rabbit, you are JUST
like your father," Mrs. Rabbit
said, smiling. She knew Peter's
dad would have been very proud
of his son's adventures!

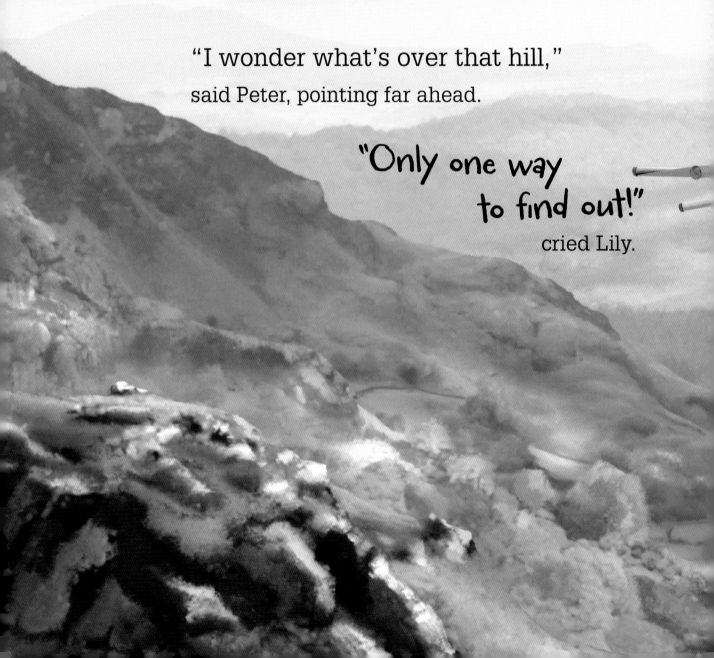

The flying machine soared across the lake
and through the valley.

"I wonder what's over that hill,"
said Peter, pointing far ahead.

"Only one way
to find out!"
cried Lily.

The three friends laughed and then shouted together,

"Life is one BIG adventure . . . LET'S GO!"

FANTASTIC FLYING MACHINE

Benjamin's dad is a very clever inventor. His flying machine was his best invention EVER, and MY dad was the first to fly it! Here's a sketch and notes from Dad's journal.

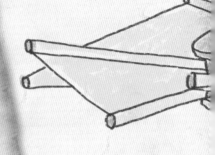

TEST PILOT'S LOG

MAXIMUM FLYING HEIGHT:	Higher than sky-high Squirrel Camp!
TOP SPEED:	Faster than Old Brown can fly (hopefully!)
FIRST FLIGHT:	A breezy Tuesday in July
LAST FLIGHT:	The same breezy Tuesday in July

NOTES: Flight abandoned when wing got caught in Mr. McGregor's plum tree, causing machine to crash. (Mr. Bouncer was NOT happy!)

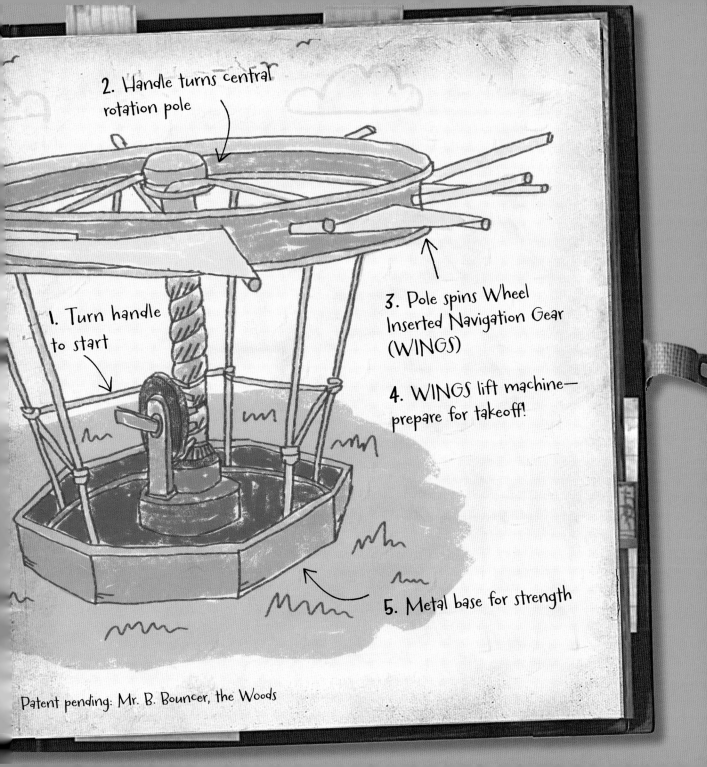

2. Handle turns central rotation pole

3. Pole spins Wheel Inserted Navigation Gear (WINGS)

1. Turn handle to start

4. WINGS lift machine— prepare for takeoff!

5. Metal base for strength

Patent pending: Mr. B. Bouncer, the Woods

TREMENDOUS Teamwork

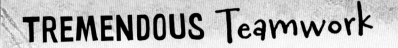

We would never have been able to put my dad's flying machine together again if we hadn't worked as a team!

Can you and your friends work together to create your own fabulous flying machine?

Here's how:

- All decide what your flying machine will look like.
- Draw and decorate your flying machine together.
- Take turns telling stories about where you'll go in your fabulous flying machine!

CONGRATULATIONS!
SKILL IN TEAMWORK CERTIFICATE

Awarded to

Age

<u>Peter, Lily, and Benjamin</u>
BEST TEAM IN THE WOODS!

Brilliant teamwork,
FRIEND!